Conejito

A FOLKTALE FROM PANAMA

Margaret Read MacDonald

Illustrated by Geraldo Valério

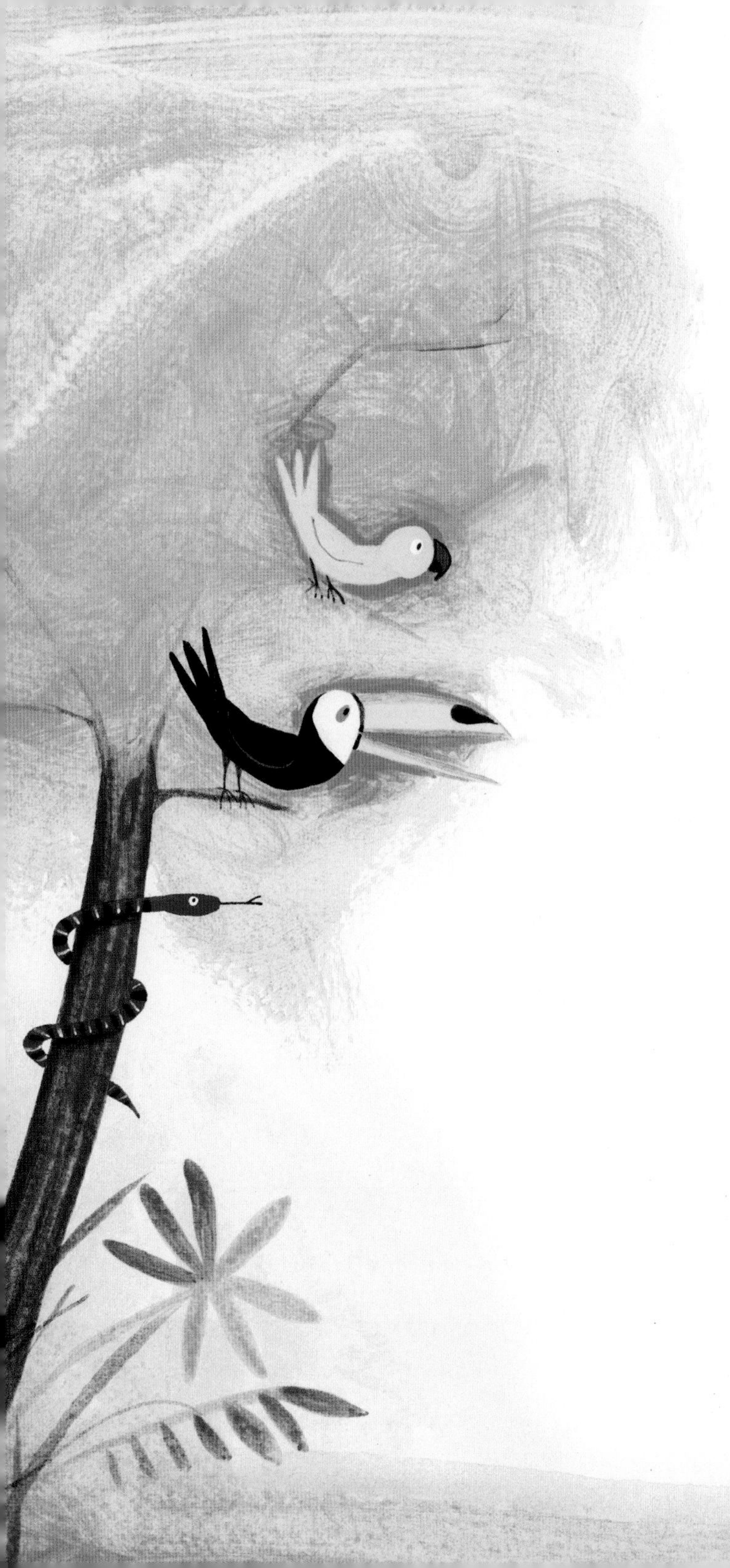

August House LittleFolk
ATLANTA

SCHOOL

Mamá said to Little Bunny,

"Conejito, my little bunny.
Vacation time is here.
You can go up the mountain
to visit your auntie, Tía Mónica.
She will feed you cakes and cookies
and every good thing . . .
until you are *¡Gordito! ¡Gordito! ¡Gordito!*
Fat! Fat! Fat!"

So Conejito went up the mountain,
dancing and leaping . . .
bailando y saltando.

"I have a sweet old auntie,
my Tía Mónica!
And when she goes out dancing . . .
they all say, 'Ooo la la!'"

And running along and singing,
not looking where he was going . . .

WHUNK!

Conejito ran right into . . .
Señor Zorro! Mr. Fox!

"Conejito!" said Señor Zorro.
"I think I have just met my LUNCH!"

"No! No! No!" cried Conejito. "You don't want to eat me!
Look how skinny I am. *¡Flaquito! ¡Flaquito! ¡Flaquito!*
Wait until I come back from Tía Mónica's house.
She is going to feed me cakes and cookies and every good thing
until I am *¡Gordito! ¡Gordito! ¡Gordito!*"

"Why not?" said Señor Zorro. *"¡Cómo no!*
I'll eat you when you come back."

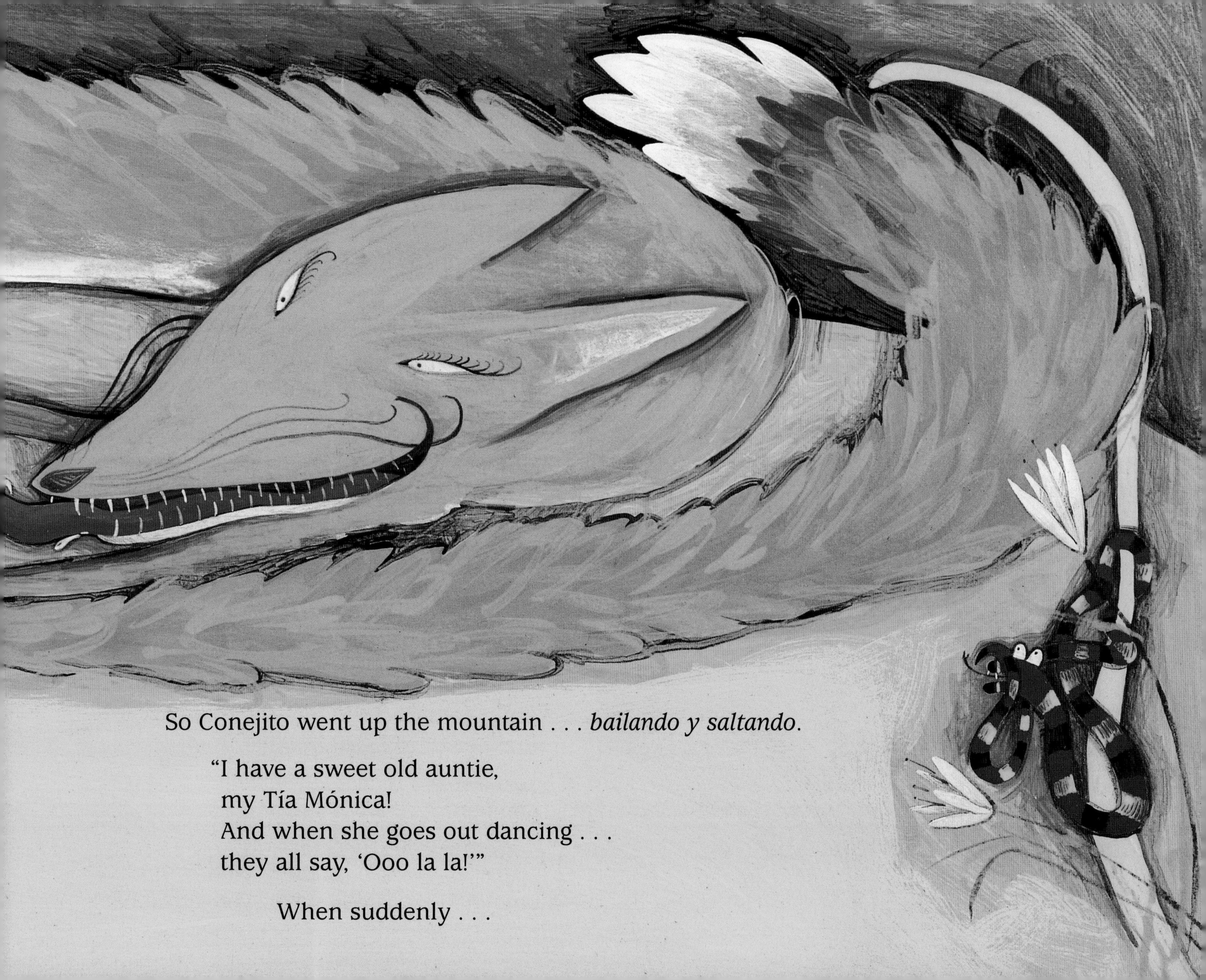

So Conejito went up the mountain . . . *bailando y saltando*.

"I have a sweet old auntie,
my Tía Mónica!
And when she goes out dancing . . .
they all say, 'Ooo la la!'"

When suddenly . . .

WHUNK!

He ran right into . . . Señor Tigre! Mr. Tiger!

"Conejito!" said Señor Tigre. "I think I have just met my LUNCH!"

"No! No! No!" cried Conejito. "You don't want to eat me!
Look how skinny I am. *¡Flaquito! ¡Flaquito! ¡Flaquito!*
Wait until I come back from Tía Mónica's house.
I will be *¡Gordito! ¡Gordito! ¡Gordito!*"

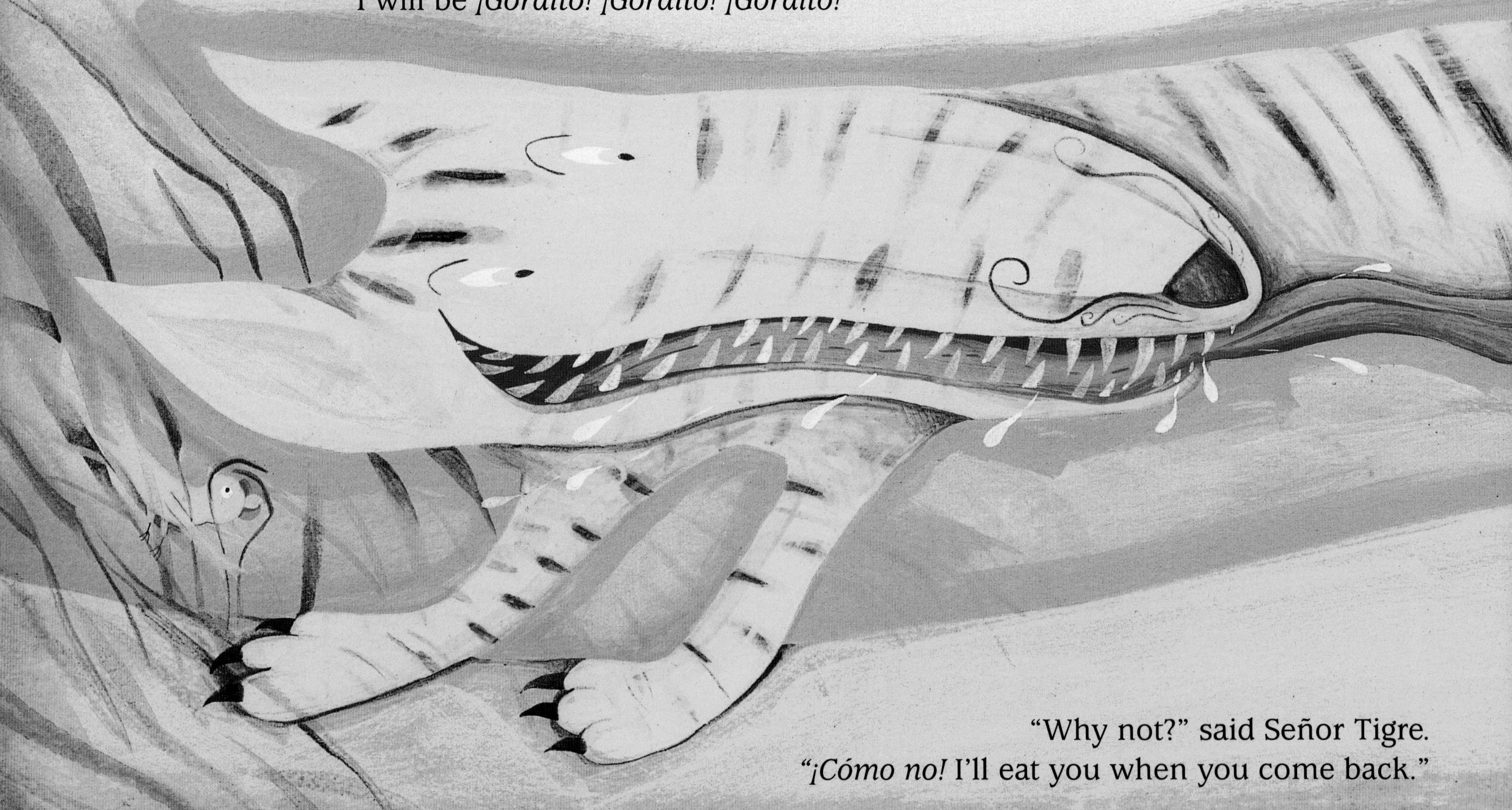

"Why not?" said Señor Tigre.
"*¡Cómo no!* I'll eat you when you come back."

So Conejito went up the mountain . . . *bailando y saltando*.

"I have a sweet old auntie,
my Tía Mónica!
And when she goes out dancing . . .
they all say, 'Ooo la la!'"

When suddenly . . .

WHUNK!

He ran right into . . . Señor León! Mr. Lion!

“Conejito!” said Señor León. “I think I have just met my LUNCH!”

“No! No! No!” cried Conejito. “You don’t want to eat me!
Look how skinny I am. *¡Flaquito! ¡Flaquito! ¡Flaquito!*
Wait until I come back from Tía Mónica’s house.
I will be *¡Gordito! ¡Gordito! ¡Gordito!”*

“Why not?” said Señor León.
“¡Cómo no! I’ll eat you when
you come back.”

So Conejito went up the mountain . . . *bailando y saltando*.

"I have a sweet old auntie,
my Tía Mónica!
And when she goes out dancing . . .
they all say, 'Ooo la la!'"

When suddenly . . .

WHUNK!

He ran right into . . . Tía Mónica!

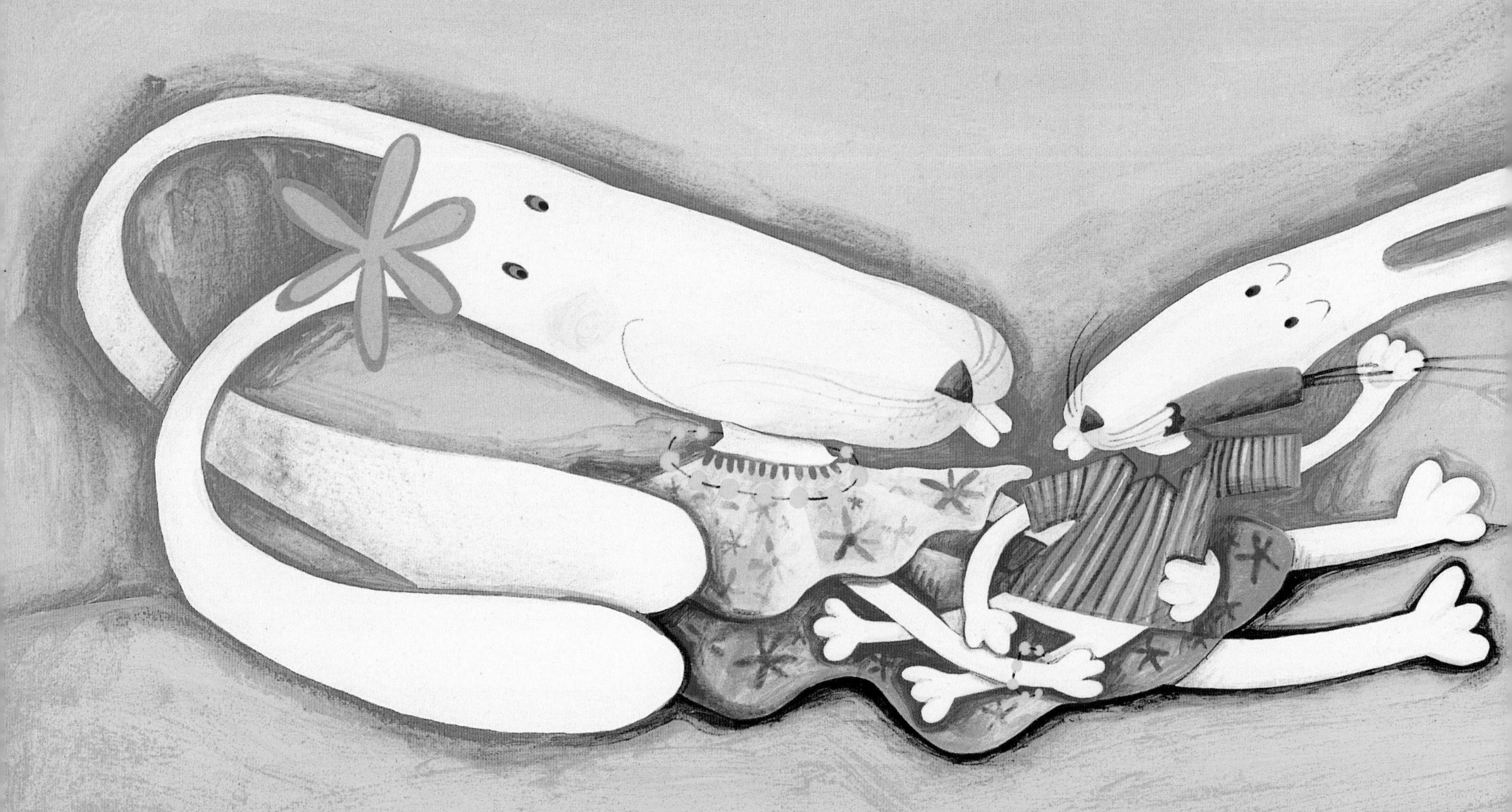

"Oh, my little Conejito! Did you come to stay with me?"

"Yes, I did!" said Conejito.
"Are you going to feed me cakes and cookies and every good thing?
Until I am *¡Gordito! ¡Gordito! ¡Gordito!*"

“Yes, I am,” said his auntie.
“But I am also going to feed you fruits and vegetables
and fresh mountain water
until you are strong! Strong! Strong!”

So Conejito ate and played and ate and played on the mountaintop
until he was healthy and strong and fat as a butterball!

How Conejito and his auntie did dance!

"I have a sweet old auntie,
my Tía Mónica!
And when she goes out dancing . . .
they all say, 'Ooo la la!'"

Soon it was time for Conejito to go home to his mamá.

"Tía Mónica, I am afraid to go back down the mountain,
I met a fox.
I met a tiger.
I met a lion.
They all want to eat me for lunch!"

“Don’t let those bullies bother you!” said his auntie.
“Just pop inside this barrel.

You can roll right down the mountain.

Roll right past Señor León.

Roll right past Señor Tigre.

Roll right past Señor Zorro.

Roll right to your mamá’s house!

I’m going to build a big smoky fire up here.
If they stop you, tell them the mountain is on fire
and they had better run away fast.”

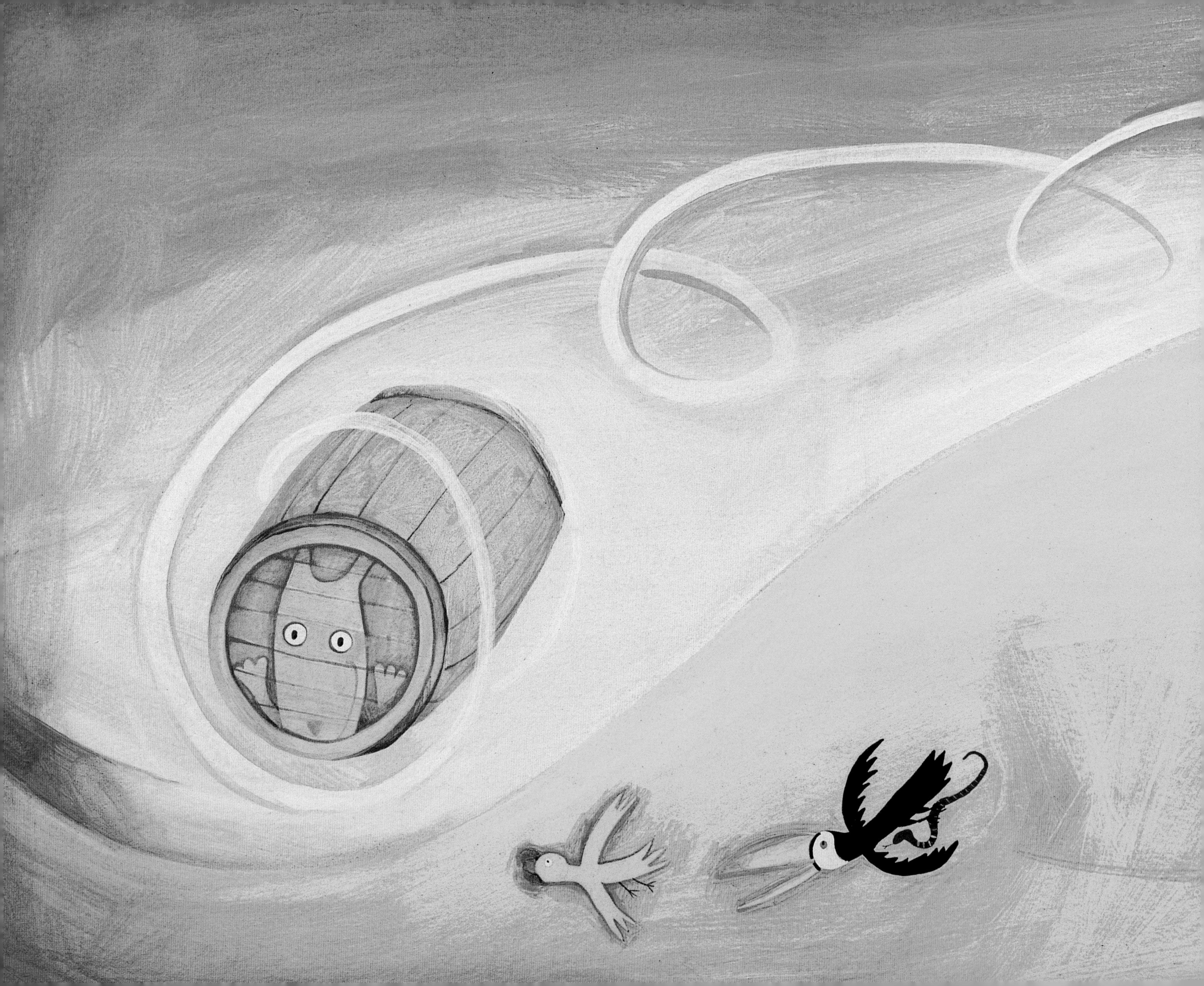

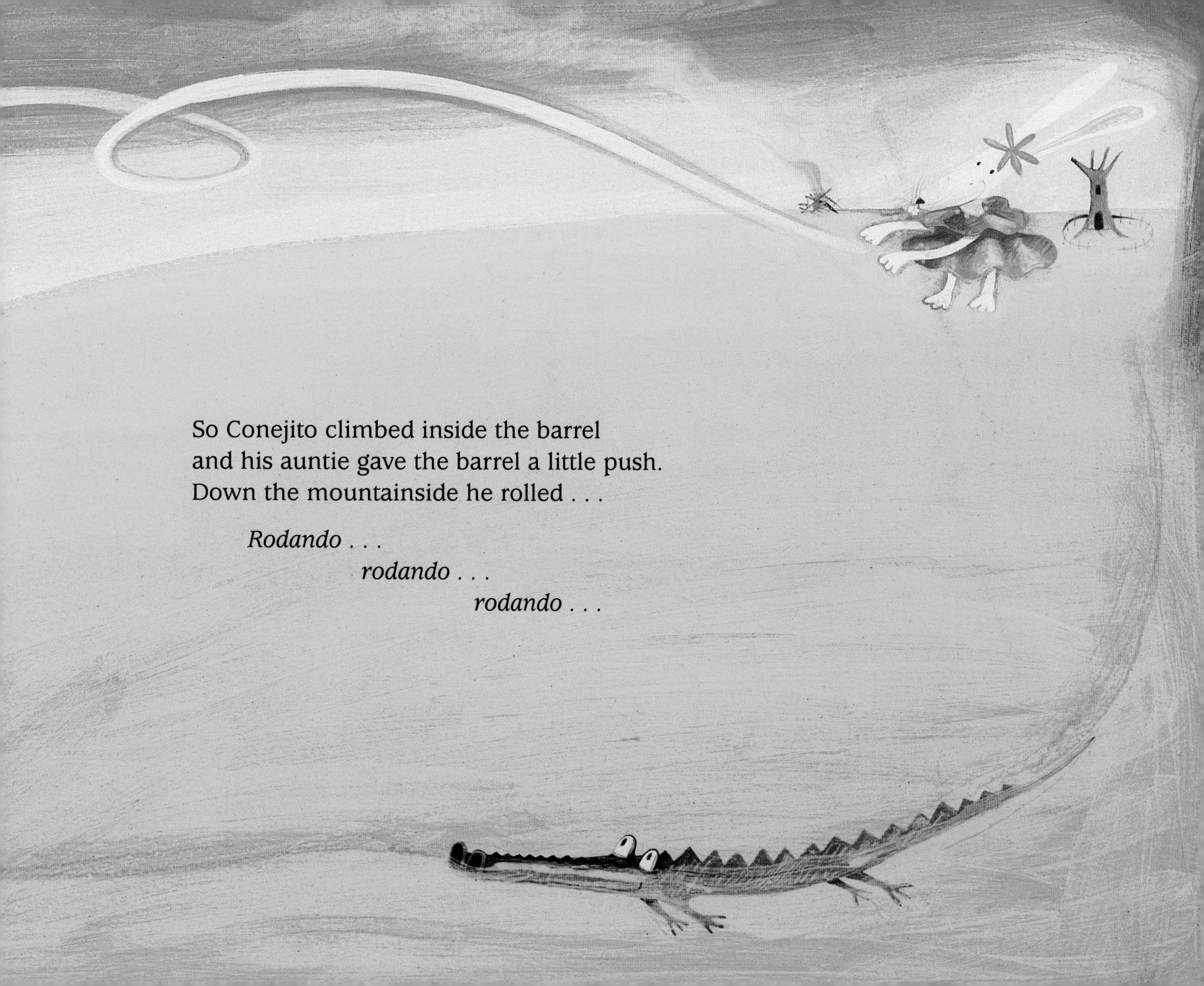

So Conejito climbed inside the barrel
and his auntie gave the barrel a little push.
Down the mountainside he rolled . . .

Rodando . . .

rodando . . .

rodando . . .

WHUNK!
Right into Señor León.

"¡Barrilito! ¡Barrilito!
Have you seen Conejito?
Little Barrel! Little Barrel!
Have you seen Conejito?"

From inside the barrel,
Conejito called out:
"The mountain's on fire!
Conejito is, too!
Run quick, Señor León—
or you'll be barbecue!"

Senor León thought
the mountain was really on fire.
He ran away so fast.
Huyendo . . . huyendo . . . huyendo . . .
and he was gone!

On down the hill rolled Conejito in his barrel.

Rodando . . .

rodando . . .

rodando . . .

WHUNK!

Right into Señor Tigre.

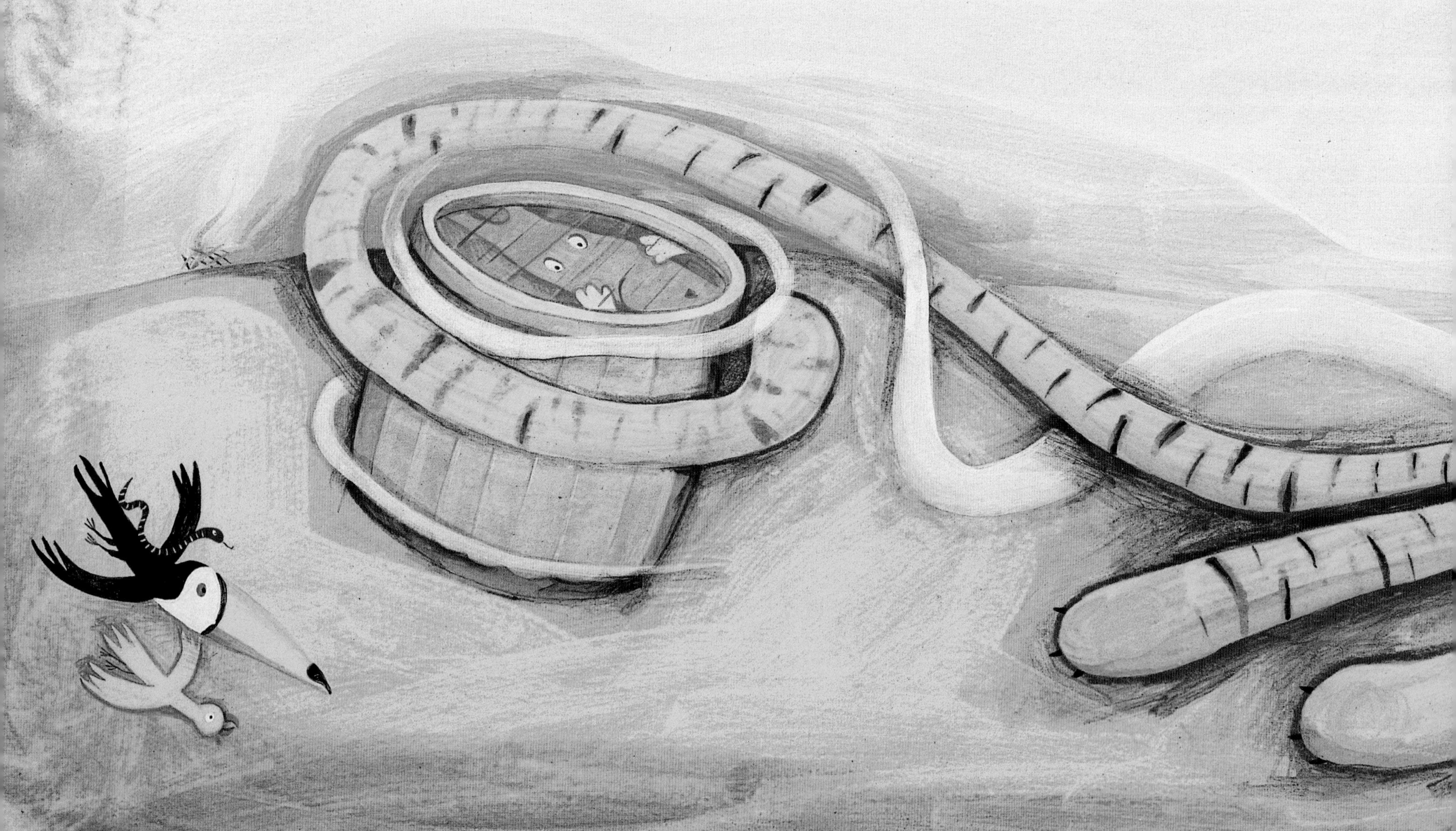

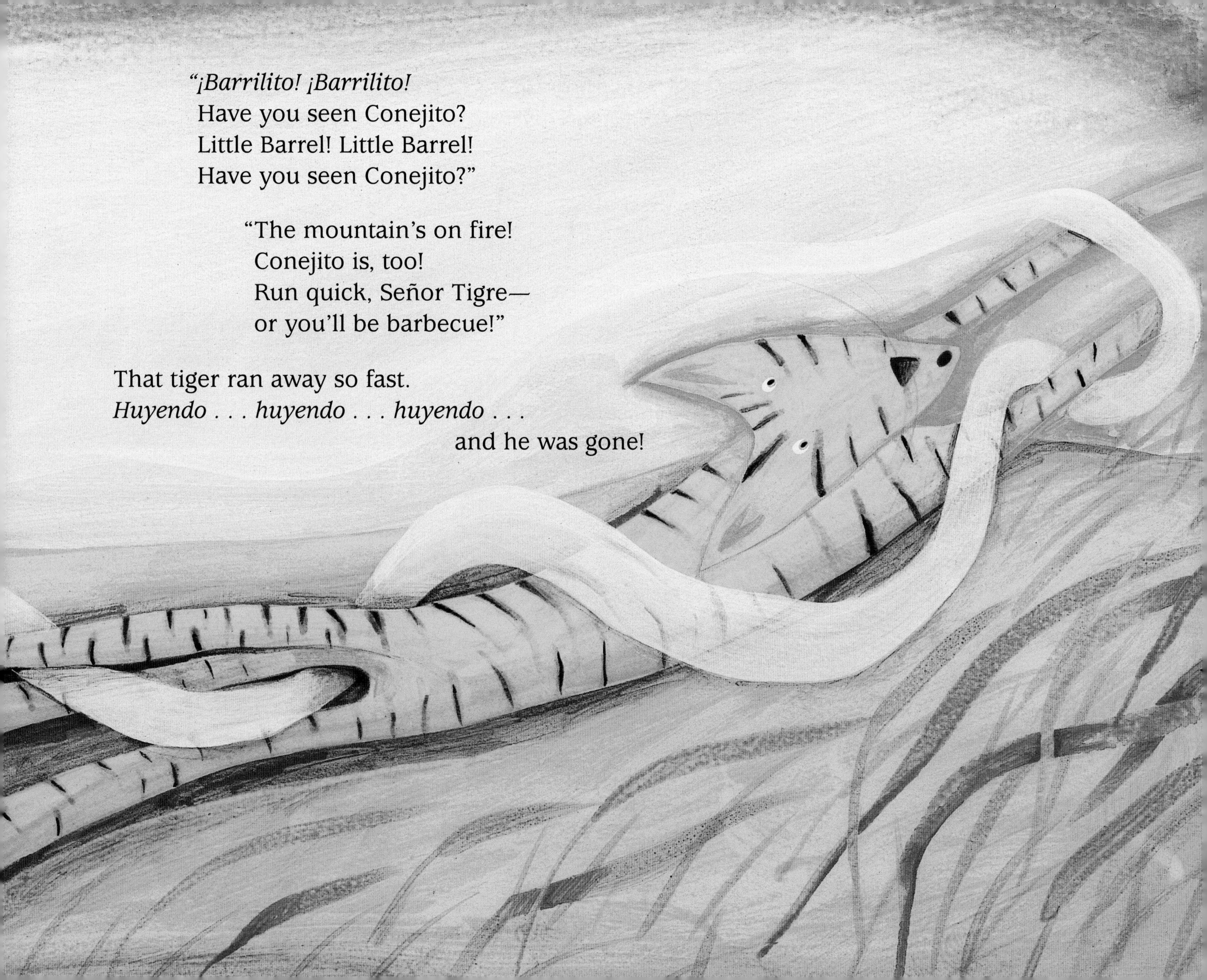

"¡Barrilito! ¡Barrilito!
Have you seen Conejito?
Little Barrel! Little Barrel!
Have you seen Conejito?"

"The mountain's on fire!
Conejito is, too!
Run quick, Señor Tigre—
or you'll be barbecue!"

That tiger ran away so fast.
Huyendo . . . huyendo . . . huyendo . . .
and he was gone!

Down the mountain rolled Conejito.

Rodando . . .

rodando . . .

rodando . . .

WHUNK!

Right into Señor Zorro.

"¡Barrilito! ¡Barrilito!

Have you seen Conejito?

Little Barrel! Little Barrel!

Have you seen Conejito?"

“The mountain’s on fire!
Conejito is, too!
Run quick, Señor Zorro—
or you’ll be barbecue!”

Off ran the fox. *Huyendo . . . huyendo . . . huyendo* . . . and he was gone!

Down the mountain rolled Conejito.

Rodando . . . rodando . . . rodando . . .

Down the mountain until . . . WHUNK!

Conejito's barrel whomped into his own mamá!

"*¡Barrilito! ¡Barrilito!* Have you seen Conejito?
Little Barrel! Little Barrel! Have you seen Conejito?"

From inside the barrel, Conejito called out, "Mamá! It's me!"

His mamá pulled off the lid, and out hopped Conejito!

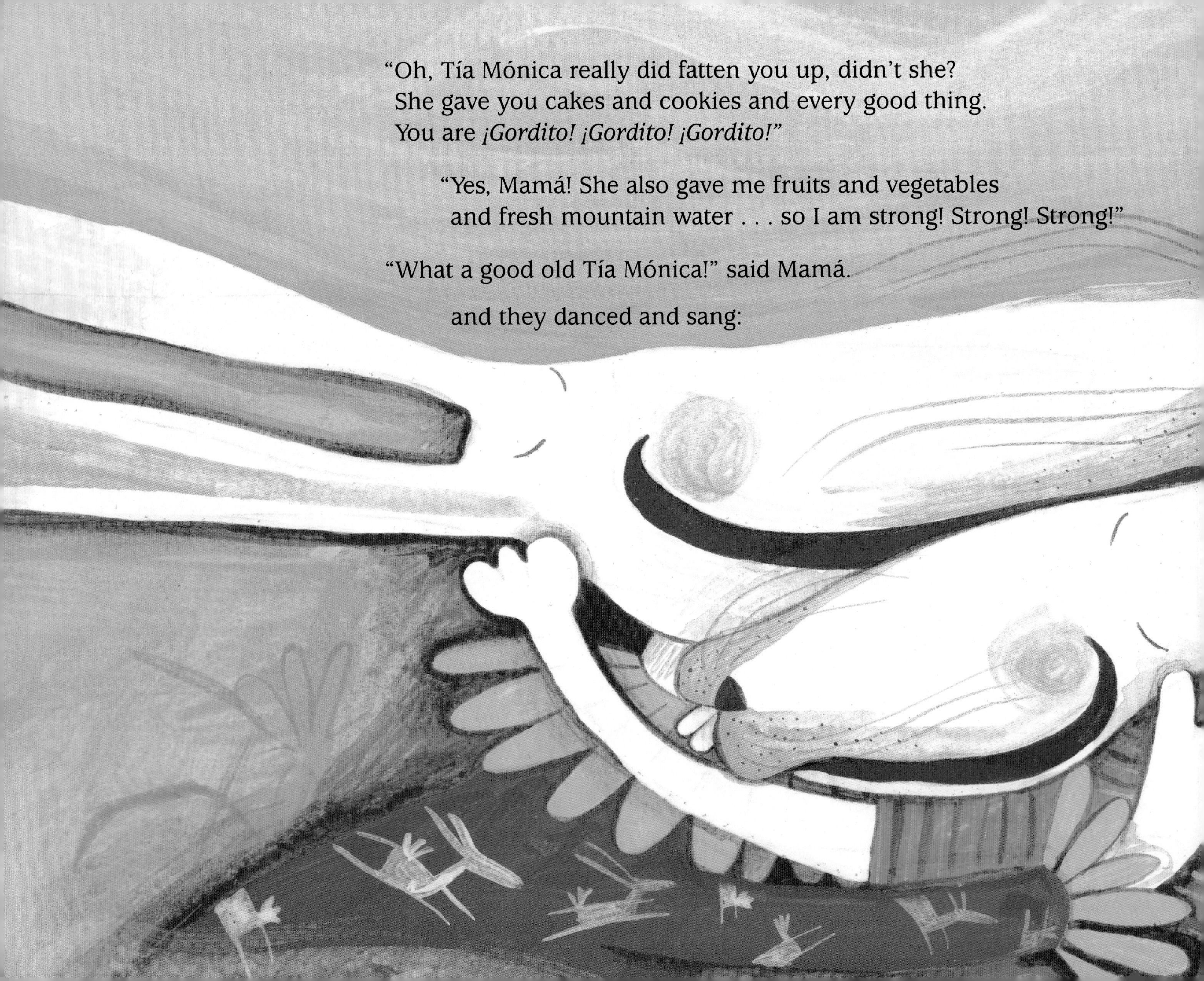

“Oh, Tía Mónica really did fatten you up, didn’t she?
She gave you cakes and cookies and every good thing.
You are *¡Gordito! ¡Gordito! ¡Gordito!”*

“Yes, Mamá! She also gave me fruits and vegetables
and fresh mountain water . . . so I am strong! Strong! Strong!”

“What a good old Tía Mónica!” said Mamá.

and they danced and sang:

We have a sweet old aunt - ie, our Tí - a Món - i - ca, and
Te - ne - mos u - na Tí - a, La Tí - a Món - i - ca, y
when she goes out danc - ing, they all say, ‘Ooo la la!’
cuan - do sale a bai - lar, de - ci - mos, ‘¡Ooo la la!’

For Baby Cordelia Skye Whitman,
whose *mamá* and *papá* are *bailando y saltando* with joy—MRM

For Nicoli and Igor—GV

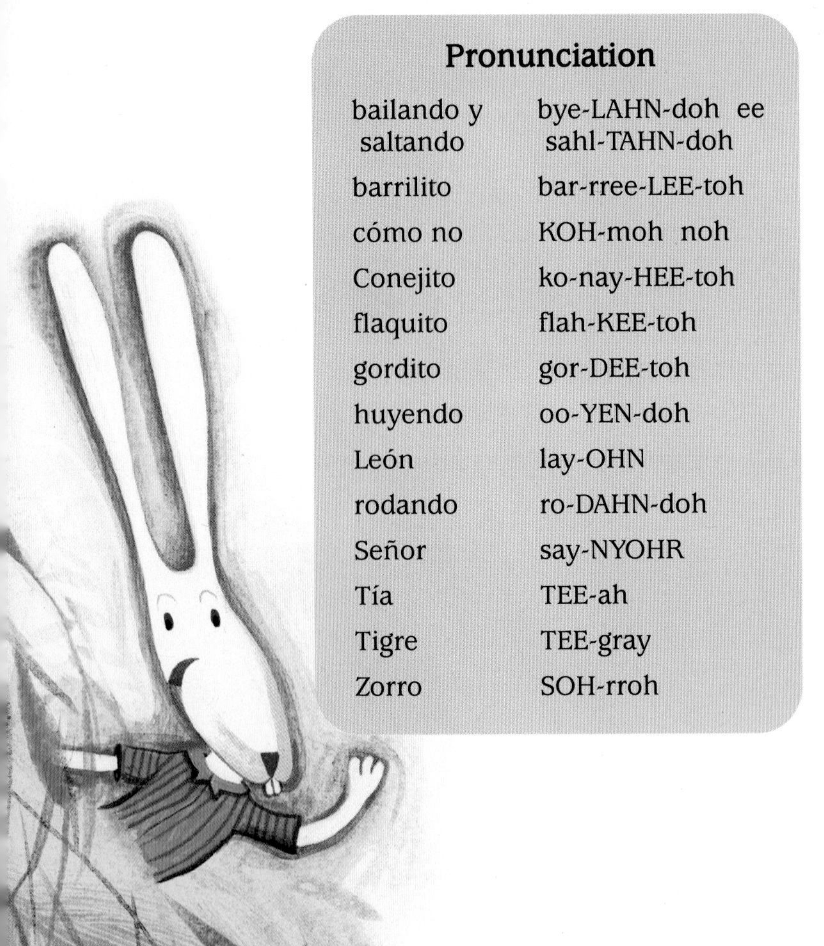

Pronunciation

bailando y saltando	bye-LAHN-doh ee sahl-TAHN-doh
barrilito	bar-rree-LEE-toh
cómo no	KOH-moh noh
Conejito	ko-nay-HEE-toh
flaquito	flah-KEE-toh
gordito	gor-DEE-toh
huyendo	oo-YEN-doh
León	lay-OHN
rodando	ro-DAHN-doh
Señor	say-NYOHR
Tía	TEE-ah
Tigre	TEE-gray
Zorro	SOH-rroh

Published 2006 by August House LittleFolk. Atlanta
augusthouse.com

Book design by Joy Freeman
Manufactured in Korea

Author's Note:
This story is retold from "El Conejito" in the collection, *El Conejito: Narrativa Oral Panameña* by Rogelio Sinán, illus. Jorge Korea (Editorial Universitaria Centroamericana), pp. 7–14. I have introduced into the story a dancing song that I learned at a Girl Scout camp in Puerto Rico in 1963.

10 9 8 7 6 5 4 3 2 1 PB
LIBRARY OF CONGRESS CATALOGING-IN-PUBLICATION DATA
MacDonald, Margaret Read, 1940–
Conejito : a folktale from Panama / Margaret Read MacDonald ; illustrated by Geraldo Valério.
p. cm.
Summary: In this folktale from Panama, a little rabbit and his Tía Monica outwit a fox, a tiger, and a lion, all of whom want to eat him for lunch.
ISBN: 978-1-939160-96-6 (paperback)
[1. Folklore—Panama.] I. Valério, Geraldo, ill. II. Title.
PZ8.1.M15924Con 2006
398.2′0972287′0452932—dc22
[E] 2005052567

The paper used in this publication meets the minimum requirements of the American National Standards for Information Sciences—Permanence of Paper for Printed Library Materials, ANSI.48–1984.